I Like Monkeys because...

11

For Cooper
P.H.

For all the monkeys at Twycross Zoo,
including Janet, Malcolm and Betty

First published 1993 by Walker Books Ltd
87 Vauxhall Walk, London SE11 5HJ

This edition published 2010

2 4 6 8 10 9 7 5 3 1

Text © 1993 Peter Hansard
Illustrations © 1993 Pat Casey

The moral rights of the author and illustrator
have been asserted

This book has been typeset in Bembo Educational

Printed in China

British Library Cataloguing in Publication Data:
a catalogue record for this book is available from the British Library

ISBN 978-1-4063-1858-6

www.walker.co.uk

I Like Monkeys because...

Peter Hansard

illustrated by Pat Casey

WALKER BOOKS
AND SUBSIDIARIES
LONDON · BOSTON · SYDNEY · AUCKLAND

Now when the sun comes up
it's hungry monkey time.

Time to look for fruit and leaves.
Time for breakfast on a branch.

I like monkeys because…
I like the way they huddle.
I like the way they cuddle.

I like the way they clean each
other's fur.

I like monkeys because…
I like the funny way they play.
Young ones tease and trick, then
scamper off as fast as they can go.

I like monkeys because…
I like the way they jump
from branch to branch,
from tree to tree.

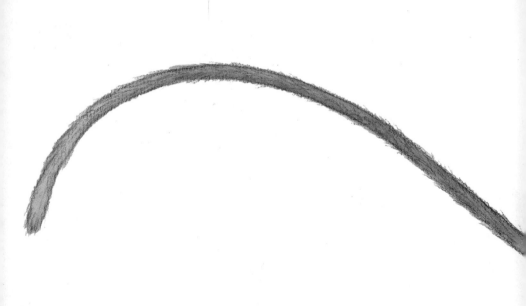

What a **mighty** leap!

Some monkeys' tails are
longer than their bodies.

Some monkeys talk by making faces.
They flash their eyebrows and waggle
their tongues. I wonder what they're
saying?

A monkey's paw is a little hand
with tiny fingernails.

I like baby monkeys because...

They scream and rush about and leap and scold and shriek and

wave their arms
and pull and tug
and cause all sorts of bother.

Mother carries baby
tucked up underneath

or riding piggyback.
Baby knows to hang on tight.

This monkey is beautiful and black and white and hairy.

This monkey has a bald head.

These monkeys have long noses.

Now when the sun is high
it's lazy monkey time.
Time to have some lunch.
Time to stretch and yawn.
Time to groom and chatter.

These are tiny Squirrel monkeys.

These are big Baboons.

These monkeys keep nice and
warm in their volcanic pool.
Can you think of a better way
to spend a snowy afternoon?

These young apes think the rain
is just a pain.

Orang-utans don't like water.

This Gorilla is the **biggest** ape of all.

Now when the sun is setting
it's time to settle down.

Time to make a nest of leaves.
Time to cuddle up and snooze.

The monkeys in this book

Squirrel monkeys
*live in tropical forests
and rainforests.*

Gorillas
are especially gentle.

Diana monkeys
*have a wide range of alarm calls, with
different sounds for different predators.*

Rhesus monkeys
*are tough and adaptable.
They've even been sent
into space.*

Mona monkeys
carry their food in cheek pouches.

Male Proboscis monkeys
*have large, fleshy noses which turn red
when they're angry or excited.*

Baboons
*scare their predators by flashing their eyelids,
showing their teeth, yawning and making gestures.*

Uakari monkeys
prefer to live near rivers and lakes.

Spectacled langurs
have bright orange babies.

Red-eared guenons
*are in danger of extinction
in the wild.*

Chimpanzees
*sleep in the
tree tops.*

Black-and-white colobus monkeys
*are hard to spot in trees. Their fur looks like
hanging moss.*

Spider monkeys
use their tails to help them balance. When they walk, their long arms practically drag on the ground.

Orang-utan
"Orang-utan" means "man of the forest" in Malay.

Japanese macaques
like to bathe in warm water.

Hanuman monkeys
are sacred in India.

Index

There are 10 titles in the
READ AND DISCOVER series.
Which ones have you read?

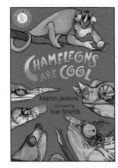
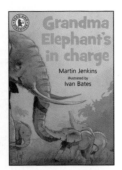
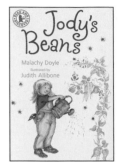

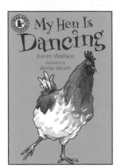

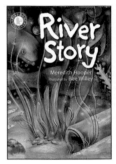

Available from all good booksellers